My Best Friend Moved Away

by Nancy Carlson

SOLD

Carolrhoda Books • Minneapolis

Carolrhoda Books
A division of Lerner Publishing Group, Inc.
241 First Avenue North
Minneapolis, MN 55401 U.S.A.

Website address: www.lernerbooks.com

Library of Congress Cataloging-in-Publication Data Available.
ISBN: 978–0–7613–8954–5 (pbk. : alk. paper)
ISBN: 978–0–7613–8960–6 (eBook)

Manufactured in the United States of America

2-33614-12538-4/14/2016

To our old neighbors,
the Coronnas

My best friend and I did everything together.

But then she moved away.

Now the neighborhood seems so quiet.

Will I ever have a best friend again?

My best friend and I knew
each other when we were babies.

We started kindergarten,

and grade school together.

But then she moved away. Now I will
have to go to school all by myself.

My best friend and I always had
so much fun hanging out in our fort,

exploring new galaxies,

or playing soccer.

But then she moved away. Now I will
be bored for the rest of my life.

My best friend and I sometimes got in fights,

but we always made up.

Now that she moved away I
have no one to say I'm sorry to.

My best friend and I shared everything, like secrets,

Halloween candy, and even

the chicken pox!

Now that she moved away, who will I share things with?

A new family is moving into my best friend's house.

They have a dog . . .

and toys . . .

and someone who looks my age!

My best friend moved away,

and I'm sure going to miss her.

But I know she'll make new friends—
just like me!